Learning to Read, Step by Step!

Ready to Read   Preschool–Kindergarten
• big type and easy words • rhyme and rhythm • picture clues
For children who know the alphabet and are eager to
begin reading.

Reading with Help   Preschool–Grade 1
• basic vocabulary • short sentences • simple stories
For children who recognize familiar words and sound out
new words with help.

Reading on Your Own   Grades 1–3
• engaging characters • easy-to-follow plots • popular topics
For children who are ready to read on their own.

Reading Paragraphs   Grades 2–3
• challenging vocabulary • short paragraphs • exciting stories
For newly independent readers who read simple sentences
with confidence.

Ready for Chapters   Grades 2–4
• chapters • longer paragraphs • full-color art
For children who want to take the plunge into chapter books
but still like colorful pictures.

STEP INTO READING® is designed to give every child a successful
reading experience. The grade levels are only guides; children will progress
through the steps at their own speed, developing confidence in their reading.

Remember, a lifetime love of reading starts with a single step!

The editors would like to thank Jim Breheny, Director, Bronx Zoo, and EVP of WCS Zoos & Aquarium, New York, for his assistance in the preparation of this book.

Visit us on the Web!
StepIntoReading.com
randomhousekids.com

Educators and librarians, for a variety of teaching tools, visit us at
RHTeachersLibrarians.com

ISBN 978-1-101-93906-2 (trade) — ISBN 978-1-101-93907-9 (lib. bdg.) — ISBN 978-1-101-93908-6 (ebook)

Printed in the United States of America
10 9 8 7 6 5 4 3 2 1

Wild Winter Creatures!

by Martin Kratt and Chris Kratt

Random House ⌂ New York

And . . . *brrr* . . .
we're finding out
how to stay warm with
cold-weather creatures.

Many animals live
in cold climates.
They have amazing
Creature Powers
to help them survive
in the ice and snow!

They have one or more of the 3 *F*s.

Oh yeah, the 3 *F*s.

FUR

FEATHERS

FAT

They help keep creatures
that live in the cold warm.

Let's meet some winter creatures . . .
. . . and activate Creature Powers!

Snowy Owl!

Snowy owls have feathers
as white as the snow.

They keep owls warm.

Snowy owls even have
feathers on their toes.
That's really good
for standing in the snow.

Polar Bear!

Polar bears have thick coats
of very warm fur.
They walk in the snow,
sleep in the snow,
and play in the snow!

Polar bears swim
in icy water.
Then they shake their
bodies to dry out
and fluff their fur.

Walrus!

Walruses are big-bodied.
They have layers of fat
called blubber.
It keeps them warm
in icy water.

Walruses can look pink
when blood travels to their skin
to let off excess heat!

Snowshoe Hare and Ermine!

In summer, snowshoe hares have brown fur.

So do ermines.

The ermine is a member of the weasel family.

As winter approaches,

their fur turns white!

This helps both creatures

blend in with the snow

when they hunt and hide.

Lynx!

Lynxes have wide, flat feet
that help them run
on top of the snow.
They chase prey
such as snowshoe hares.

However, snowshoe hares
also have giant feet,
so they can run away!

Big feet
don't sink into
the snow.

Musk Ox!

Musk oxen have long, shaggy fur coats to keep them very warm. Musk ox calves snuggle inside the herd for extra warmth.

Musk oxen form a circle
to protect themselves
from wolves.

"Calves in the middle,"
says Chris.

"Horns out!" says Martin.

Penguin!

Penguins are covered
with smooth feathers.
The feathers keep
them warm.

These feathers also
help them swim fast
in cold water.
Penguins have to be speedy
to escape leopard seals!

Winter Birds!

Many birds fly to warmer climates in the winter. Some do not.

Birds in cold climates puff out their feathers to hold warm air close to their bodies.

They find food
in different ways.
Blue jays and woodpeckers
dig up nuts and seeds.
Woodpeckers also make
holes in trees to get
to the insects inside.

River Otter!

River otters have waterproof fur coats to keep them warm.

In the water, they catch fish.

River otters love
to slide down hills.
They use their bellies as sleds.
They use a fourth *F* to stay
warm . . .

Fun!

Under the Snow!

Some animals use the snow for protection.

Voles and other small animals make tunnels under the snow.

There they are much safer from predators like snowy owls and lynxes.

"Whoa! This is fun,"
says Chris.

"It's like a snow fort!"

Deep Sleep!

Some animals survive by sleeping through most of the winter.

we've got to keep moving
to stay warm.
Good thing there are
always more creatures
to check out!